DOUBLE TROUBLE
Dream Date

MICHAEL J. PELLOWSKI

digital cover illustration by Michael Petty
inside illustrations by Mel Crawford

To Morgan, Matt, Melanie, and Marty

Second printing by Willowisp Press 1997.

Published by PAGES Publishing Group
801 94th Avenue North, St. Petersburg, Florida 33702

Cover design and illustrations © 1997 by PAGES Publishing Group.

Printed in the United States of America

Willowisp Press®

2 4 6 8 10 9 7 5 3

ISBN 0-87406-829-0

CHAPTER One

I was sprawled across my bed reading a super-sad romance novel when the phone rang in the hallway. I sniffed and wiped away a tear. I'd have to wait a while to find out whether Judy lived or died at the end of the book. I shut the book and started to hop off my bed. But before I could get both feet on the floor, I heard a squeal outside my door.

"I get it! I get da phone! I get it!" Trouble yelled as he thundered past my room. Trouble is the nickname my twin sister Randi and I have for our little brother, Teddy. Everyone who knows our family knows how Teddy got his nickname. He earned it! Wherever Teddy goes, he gets into trouble.

Lately, Teddy loves to play with the phone. He's

always answering it and messing up messages or hanging up on people. Once he even called Seattle, Washington, by accident, and talked to a stranger for ten whole minutes. Dad went bonkers when the phone bill came, but he didn't even punish Teddy. Dad said Teddy was just a baby and that he didn't know any better. Sometimes it didn't seem fair. I knew if Randi or I made a call to Seattle, we'd be grounded until we were thirty-five years old. But I guess I couldn't really complain too much. Mom and Dad are usually fair about punishments and stuff.

I'd learned a long time ago that it was best to let Teddy do what he wanted. It was either that, or listen to him wail for hours. If he wanted to answer the phone so badly, I'd let him. I heard the phone ring one more time and then it stopped. Any second now, Teddy would have the caller completely confused.

Don't get the wrong idea. I never let Teddy go on for very long. I had a plan that worked—most of the time. As soon as Teddy answered the phone, I'd creep up behind him and wrestle the receiver out of his hand.

"Who's on the phone, Sandi?" my sister Randi called from our bathroom. She was washing her hair. It seemed as if Randi was always washing her hair. That was probably why her blond hair had so many split ends and mine didn't.

"I don't know, but I'll find out," I said as I took off my glasses and laid them on my pink bedspread near my novel. I went out into the hallway and headed toward the phone. Teddy was standing with his back to me. He had the phone pressed against his ear. Just as I reached out to grab the phone, Teddy started screaming.

"Dweeb date? What you mean, dweeb date? Ranee no got a dweeb date!" Teddy yelled. "Dweeb date! Dat dum!"

"Who are you talking to?" I asked my little brother.

"I talking to dweeb date," Teddy answered as he spun around to face me.

"Dweeb what?" I tried again.

"Ranee won a dweeb date," he chanted, gripping the phone tightly.

"You'd better let me talk," I said to Teddy as I put out my hand.

"No. My phone. I talking now," Teddy said as he pulled away from me.

"Please give me that phone," I said, trying not to get mad at him.

"No!" Teddy argued. He made a funny face by wrinkling up his nose. I loved my little brother, but I was running out of patience.

"Give me that phone," I said as I grabbed for it.

"Huh-uh," Teddy replied as we played tug of war with the phone cord. We pulled and yanked. For a kid who wasn't even four years old yet, Teddy sure was strong.

"Otay," Teddy said and suddenly let go. I toppled backward and fell splat on the floor. "Uh-oh, Sanee fall down." I looked up at him. He had the biggest devilish grin on his face. "You otay?" he asked.

"Yeah, I otay!" I grumbled as I stayed seated and lifted the phone to my ear. "Hello," I said. "This is

Sandi Daniels. Can I help you?"

"I sure hope so," a man said. "I almost hung up. I thought some kids were playing a prank on me."

"Sorry, sir," I said as I glanced at Trouble. "But my little brother answered the phone and he's just a baby."

"I notta baby!" Teddy grunted as he stamped his foot on the floor. "Sanee the baby!"

"Shh!" I said to him.

"I'd like to speak to Randi Daniels," the man said to me. "Are you her sister?"

"Yes, I am," I answered. "We're identical twins. Randi can't come to the phone. Can I take a message for her?" I didn't want to tell a stranger that Randi was washing her hair.

"Well, I wanted to give her the good news, but I guess telling her twin is almost like talking to Randi. Right?" he asked.

"Yeah, sort of," I said, thinking how perfect his question was. Randi and I had switched places so many times that it was hard to remember who we were sometimes.

We do have a couple of differences that help people tell us apart. Randi loves to wear red. My favorite colors are pink and purple. Randi loves sports and her eyesight is perfect. I don't really care about sports and I have to wear glasses or contacts.

"My name is Ken Starr," the man went on. "Do you know who I am?"

I thought for a minute. *Ken Starr?* His name sounded familiar, but I couldn't figure out who he was.

"I think so, but I'm not sure . . .," I began.

"It's okay," the man interrupted. "How about the name Eric St. John? Do you know who he is?"

"ERIC ST. JOHN!" I sputtered. "Of course, I've heard of him!"

Eric St. John was the hottest singing star around. Eric was only thirteen, but he was popular all over the world. Fan magazines plastered pictures of him all over their covers.

"Ken Starr? Now I remember who you are, Mr. Starr," I said. "You're Eric St. John's manager."

"That's right, Randi," he replied.

"Sandi," I corrected.

"Oh. Right. Sorry," Mr. Starr apologized. "Tell me, Sandi, did you enter the 'Win a Dream Date with Eric St. John' contest, too?"

"No, I didn't," I admitted. "I'm a little too grown up for dating contests. And there's only a chance in a zillion of winning."

I didn't want to tell him that I probably would have entered the contest if Randi hadn't clipped out all the entry forms in our magazines before I had a chance to get my hands on them. Eric St. John was a real hunk! He had wavy brown hair and twinkling green eyes. He was definitely cuter than the cutest boys I knew—and that included Jay-Jay Smith, Wormy Wormsley, and even Chris Miles. And even better than the way Eric looked was the way he sang. He had an incredible voice.

"So the odds of winning the grand prize are a zillion to one," laughed Mr. Starr. "Well, that's why I'm calling. Randi has won the dream date with Eric."

I was speechless. I tried to say something, but

nothing came out. I guess I should have realized that Eric St. John's manager wouldn't be calling the Daniels's house unless there was some major reason. But I couldn't believe Randi had won the grand prize.

"Sanee otay?" asked Teddy as he tugged on the sleeve of my favorite purple blouse.

"Sandi? Sandi, are you there?" Mr. Starr asked.

"Yes, I'm here," I managed to say.

"Good," Mr. Starr continued. "As part of the grand prize date package, Eric St. John will come to your hometown to give a free concert and to tape his very first rock video for his new song *Hometown Girl.*"

"*Hometown Girl?*"

"Right. The music video will be taped at your neighborhood recreation center," he explained. "Everything has already been taken care of. Randi gets to pick five friends to be in the video with her and Eric St. John."

"Do sisters count?" I asked.

"Sure, Randi can choose a sister or brother to be

in it," Mr. Starr replied.

I immediately started hoping that Randi would let me be in the video with her. But there was no way that Trouble was going to be in the video. He'd turn the whole thing into a major mess.

"Eric will spend the whole weekend in your town. Randi wrote down soccer as one of her favorite hobbies, so Eric will play a soccer game with Randi and her friends. We'll tape the game and possibly use some of the tape in the video. Sound good?"

"Yeah," I agreed. "It's great. Is there anything else I should tell Randi?"

"Yep, there's lots more," Mr. Starr said. "You and your family are invited to the rehearsal for the video. You will all be treated to lunch with Eric. And there will be lots of time for Randi to get to know Eric. After all, she's won her ultimate dream date. Got all that?"

"Yes, I do," I said. "I'll tell my sister."

"Thanks, Sandi," said Mr. Starr. "And tell your parents to call me if they have any questions." I jotted down his phone number beside all the things

I was dying to tell Randi. "See you in two weeks. Good-bye," he said.

I stood there, frozen in place. I felt like the phone was stuck to the side of my head. Seconds later, Randi walked out of our room. She was wearing her red robe and fuzzy red slippers.

"Who was that?" Randi asked as she dried her hair with a towel. "Was it Jamie?"

I shook my head to let her know the caller wasn't our best friend, Jamie Collins.

"It was dweeb date," Teddy announced proudly.

"Dweeb date?" Randi asked. "What's he talking about? Did that clod Todd the Cod Jackson call here?"

Todd had developed a crush on our cousin Mandy when she was visiting. Now that she was gone, he bugged us instead.

I shook my head. "You, you won," I sputtered.

"I won what?" Randi asked. "I've never seen you act like this before, Sandi. Are you okay?"

I looked into my sister's eyes and smiled. I reached out and put my hands on Randi's shoulders. "You won . . . a dream date with . . . " I said slowly.

"What?" she asked, her eyes growing wider.

"With Eric St. John!" I screamed.

"EEEEEEK!" shrieked Randi as she jumped up and down. I grabbed her shoulders and we jumped up and down together.

"Dream date! Dream date! Dream date!" we chanted as we bounced around happily.

"Dweeb date, dweeb date," Teddy echoed as he jumped up and down. It wasn't long before our parents came scrambling up the stairs.

"What's going on here?" Dad asked. "Could you all stop bouncing for a minute and tell us what's happening. Who called?"

Randi and I tried to calm down. Even Teddy stopped. When we were all quiet, Randi pointed at the phone with a trembling hand. "That call Sandi took," Randi began. "I-I won the dream date contest."

"And Eric St. John is coming to town in two weeks to make a music video," I added. "And Randi

14

is going to be in it."

"Isn't it wonderful?" Randi exclaimed. "Imagine! Me and Eric St. John in a music video." Randi stopped. "What video?" Randi asked. "You didn't tell me about any video."

"The video is after the soccer game, the rehearsal, and the lunch," I explained.

"What soccer game?" asked Dad.

"What rehearsal?" asked Mom.

"What lunch and what video?" Randi asked.

"Okay, I'd better fill you in," I said, looking down at the notes I'd taken.

"Let's go downstairs," Mom suggested. "But first, Randi, finish drying your hair."

"Okay," Randi grumbled as she wrapped the towel turban-style around her head.

We followed Dad downstairs and got settled. Then I picked up my story. I went over all of the things Mr. Starr had told me on the phone and handed Mom and Dad Mr. Starr's phone number.

"I guess it will be okay for Randi to be in the *Hometown Girl* video," Dad said.

"Well, it sure couldn't turn out any worse than the bubble gum commercial Randi and Sandi did with Mandy in Hollywood," Mom teased.

"I liked that commercial," I said. "We were all good in it . . . even Teddy." I smiled at my brother. He smiled back.

"I'm kidding," Mom said as she winked at me.

"Wait until the kids at school hear about this," Randi said. "They'll totally freak out."

"Remember, you get to pick five friends to be in the video with you," I reminded her. "And you can pick some kids to play soccer, too."

Randi grinned. I knew she was loving the feeling of being in control.

"Let's see," she began. "I pick you and Jamie. That means I can pick three more for the video."

"How about Chris Miles?" I suggested.

"Hmmm . . . maybe," Randi said.

"I wanna be in video," Teddy shouted as he hopped off the couch.

Randi shook her head. "You're too little."

"I not little," Teddy said.

"You have to be a good dancer," I said.

"I dancer," Trouble argued. He started jumping around doing wacky dance steps around the coffee table. We all broke up in giggles. He was so funny.

"Forget it, Teddy," Randi said. "You're not going to be in the video."

Trouble stopped dancing. He made a face at Randi and headed for the stairs.

"Where are you going, Teddy?" I asked.

"Play with Hoppy," Teddy said as he started up toward his room. Hoppy was the pet frog that Teddy had found on vacation at Lake Kickapoo. Hoppy now lived in an aquarium in Teddy's bedroom.

"Maybe you should let Teddy be in the video," Dad said as soon as he was gone.

Randi looked at me. I looked at Randi. We both looked at Mom. Mom sighed.

"I don't think it's a good idea," Mom said to Dad. "Teddy can go to the rehearsals, but I don't think he should be in the video. You know all the crazy things that happen when Teddy's around."

"Okay," Dad said with a grin. "I guess you're

17

right. But there's one thing I'd like to know—who is this Eric St. John? I've never heard of him."

"Eric is totally great," Randi sighed. "And our video will make him even more famous than he already is."

"Our video?" I repeated.

"Yep," she said.

"Oh, no," I groaned as I realized Randi was already thinking of herself as the star of the show. "Here we go again!"

18

CHAPTER **TWO**

IT seemed as if Randi's news spread through the school within minutes on Monday. By lunch time, everyone knew all about the contest, the soccer game, and the video. I guess the fifteen people Randi and I had called over the weekend had helped us spread our big news.

"Congratulations, Randi," Chris Miles said as Randi, Jamie, and I walked past him in the hallway.

"Thanks, Chris," Randi said.

As we headed toward class, kids we hardly knew spoke to us or waved.

"The kids sure are friendly today," I said as I waved back at a boy I didn't even know.

"I don't think they all want to be our friends,"

Jamie said. "They just want Randi to pick them to be in the video."

"You think people would do that?" I asked. "It's pretty stupid for them to think Randi would pick them because they were nice to her for one day."

"Hi, Randi. You look really nice," a familiar voice behind us said. We all stopped and turned around. Sure enough, there stood Bobbi Joy Boikin. "Your hair looks pretty today."

I couldn't believe it. Bobbi Joy Boikin, the school bully and our biggest enemy, was being super-sweet to Randi. I looked into Bobbi Joy's freckled face. The way her frizzy red hair stood out on the sides looked scary—like she belonged in a horror movie.

"And how are you, Sandi?" Bobbi Joy asked, turning to me. "Are you ready for our spelling test? I bet you'll get an A."

"I hope so," I admitted. I didn't want to be rude, but it was strange being so polite to Bobbi Joy. I mean, she had done some pretty nasty things to us. It was hard to forget about them—even if she was being nicer than she'd ever been before.

I looked at Randi's and Jamie's faces. I could tell from their expressions that they felt the same way. Bobbi Joy didn't like us and we didn't like her.

"This is ridiculous," Jamie mumbled as she started to walk away. We followed her.

"Bye," Bobbi Joy called after us.

"Bye," I said in my sweetest voice as we turned the corner. "What next?" I grumbled.

Bump! We walked right into the class clod, Todd the Cod Jackson.

"Good morning, girls," Todd said as he grinned from ear to ear.

"Good morning, Todd," I said.

"Morning," Randi grunted matter-of-factly.

Jamie grunted her hello, too. It wasn't that we disliked Todd exactly. But he had bad manners that grossed us out most of the time. The absolute worst thing Todd did was get a crush on Randi and me after Mandy went back to Hollywood. He was always hanging around.

"Do you want something, Todd?" Jamie asked as she backed away from him. "The first bell is

going to ring pretty soon and we have to get to class."

Todd nodded. "Can I carry your books?" he asked.

"No, thanks, Todd," I said as I clutched my books tighter to me.

"Not you," Todd grunted.

"Huh?" I sputtered.

"I wasn't asking you," Todd said in the super-slow way he talked. "I want to carry Randi's books." Todd seemed to take a breath after each and every word.

Jamie struggled to keep from laughing out loud. I looked at Randi's face. I think she was in shock.

"No, thanks, Todd," Randi refused. "I like carry-ing my own books."

Todd nodded and waddled off down the hall.

"Can you believe the nerve of that Todd Jack-son?" I asked.

"Are you jealous because he's going after your famous sister?" Jamie asked.

Randi giggled. I shot Jamie a wicked look. And

then I couldn't help it. I burst out laughing, too. Soon all three of us were giggling.

"What's so funny, girls?" asked Ms. Morgan as she walked out of a nearby classroom. She was one of the best teachers in our school. We liked her a lot.

"You wouldn't believe it," I told her. "Everyone is being so nice to Randi because she won a contest. It's like Randi's dream date with Eric St. John has turned her into a celebrity, too."

"Oh, yes. I heard about it," Ms. Morgan said. "The Recreation Commission received a call from Eric's manager about using the rec center to make the video." Ms. Morgan was a member of the town's recreation commission. "We're all very excited about it. It'll certainly make our town famous."

"I'm excited, too," Randi admitted. "But it's going to be tough to pick who's going to be in the video. Everyone wants to be in it."

Ms. Morgan nodded and smiled. "Yes, if I were fifteen years younger, I'd be pestering you, too," she admitted. "That Eric St. John is a real cutie."

Just then the bell rang. "Oops. You'd better hurry and get to class," Ms. Morgan urged. "Randi may be a celebrity, but if you're late you'll get detention anyway."

We laughed and hurried down the hall to our class. As we slid into our seats, I thought about Bobbi Joy's stupid grin and Todd the Cod asking to carry Randi's books. How long was everyone going to act so phony around us? It was too weird.

♦ ♦ ♦ ♦ ♦

"So tomorrow is the big day?" Dad asked Randi two weeks later. We were in the middle of eating dinner.

"Yep, tomorrow your dream date begins," I said dramatically.

"Dweeb date," Teddy muttered as he mashed his peas into green mush with his fork.

"Those two weeks sure went fast," Mom added as she passed the gravy.

"They didn't go fast enough for me," I said as I

poured gravy onto my roast. "I'm so sick of the way all the kids are acting."

"What do you mean, Sandi?" Dad asked.

"All the kids treat Randi like she's a queen or something just because she won the contest," I explained. "I get tired of all these weird kids being super-nice and polite around her. As soon as Eric St. John goes home, they'll all be jerks again."

I took a couple bites of dinner, then went on. "And at lunch, the kids all give their desserts to Randi."

"Yeah, I've gained three whole pounds," Randi chuckled as she buttered a slice of bread.

"Boys line up to carry her books to class," I added. "And some of them even offered to do her homework for her."

Mom shot a glance in Randi's direction.

"Don't worry, Mom," Randi said. "I'm doing my own homework."

"But she never refused a dessert," I added.

"Why let great food go to waste?" Randi asked with a laugh.

"You sound a little jealous, Sandi," Dad said.

"Well, maybe I am a little," I admitted. "But I think it's really gross the way everyone says nice things to you just so you'll pick them. If I hear Bobbi Joy Boikin say 'have a nice day' one more time, I'll flip out."

Randi laughed and almost choked on the bite of bread she was chewing.

"So who did you pick to be in the video?" Mom asked.

"Sandi and Jamie and Chris Miles," Randi announced. "And I've also decided to ask Billy Parker, the captain of the soccer team, and Sylvia Rumsford."

I smiled. Randi had picked the same kids I would've picked. Good. She hadn't picked the phonies for buying her extra food. I was proud of her.

"What about the soccer game?" Dad asked. "Didn't Mr. Starr say you could pick different kids for that?"

Mom and Dad had talked to Mr. Starr to make

all the arrangements.

"I think the kids from the soccer team should be in the soccer game," Randi said logically. "They'll look the most natural. And Mr. Starr is going to pick some of the kids, too, so we'll have the right look or something."

"Tomorrow should be exciting," Dad said, glancing down at the notes he'd taken. "First you ride to the airport in a limo to meet Eric's plane. Then you come back here for some publicity pictures."

Randi sighed dreamily. "Tomorrow I meet Eric St. John," she said with a silly grin on her face. "I can't believe my dream is coming true."

CHAPTER **Three**

THE next day was crazy. Everybody was running around our house like a maniac. Jamie came over early to help Randi and me pick out the right clothes to wear to meet Eric at the airport.

We both wanted to look outstanding when we met Eric. I tried on my new pants, my favorite jeans, and a dress. None of them looked right.

Randi finally chose her denim skirt and a matching vest. With them, she wore her favorite red blouse and a red bracelet. I picked my prettiest pink dress and decided to wear my contact lenses, too.

"The perfect finishing touch would be make-up," Randi said to Mom.

"You know the rule," Mom said.

"Not till junior high," Randi and I said together.

"But, Mom," Randi groaned. "We're going to look like babies."

"Ranee's a baby! Ranee's a baby!" Teddy chanted from out in the hallway. The little twerp had been listening outside the door. I jerked open our door and Teddy tumbled into our room.

"Teddy, you shouldn't be standing out there," Mom scolded him as she picked him up. "It's not nice to listen to what other people are saying."

"And don't call me a baby," Randi warned.

"Ranee a baby and she got a dweeb date," replied Trouble as he wiggled free from Mom's arms and scampered from our room.

Jamie laughed. "Wait until Eric meets Teddy," she teased.

"Yeah, he'll jump right back on the plane before we even get to know him," I said, looking into our vanity mirror. "You're right, Randi. Makeup would help. Mom, how come Cousin Mandy gets to wear makeup if she wants to?"

"Because she's a professional actress and

because she lives in Hollywood," Mom said. "Things are different there. And besides, Mandy is not my daughter so I don't get to decide what's right for her."

I guess we both looked really disappointed. "Maybe just this once, we could make an exception to the rule," Mom said. "How about if I go get some of my blush and lipstick?"

As Mom walked out of our room, Randi and I jumped up and down and screamed.

"I can't believe Mom is letting us wear makeup," I said to Jamie and Randi. "This is great."

"Who cares about the makeup? I can't believe you're going to the airport in a limo to meet *the* Eric St. John," sighed Jamie as she flopped on my bed. "It's just too awesome for words."

"Jamie, we'd take you with us, but Mr. Starr said we could only bring our family," Randi explained. "He said they didn't want reporters and lots of kids hanging around the airport."

"Mr. Starr sure is a strange guy," I added. "I mean, he seems to decide everything for Eric. Eric can do this. He can't do that. Mr. Starr probably never lets Eric out of his sight."

"I guess that's what a manager does," Jamie said. "He's supposed to protect his client from fans."

"Protect?" Randi asked. "From the way he's keeping everything so secretive, it seems like he doesn't want anyone to see Eric until he's good and ready. Maybe he's hiding something."

"Maybe Eric is bald and wears a wig," Jamie joked.

"Or maybe he has warts," I suggested.

We all laughed.

"Okay, girls," said Mom as she spread out her makeup on the vanity. "Just remember, this is a one-time thing."

"Right, Mom," Randi said as she winked at me. We began to put on a little blush and lipstick.

After we finished, we went downstairs where Dad and Teddy were waiting. Dad whistled when he saw us. I blushed. I looked at Randi and she was turning pink, too.

"Wow! You girls look beautiful," he said. "Make sure you tell that Eric guy you're too young to date."

"Dad!" Randi said. "Stop teasing us."

"Okay, okay," said Dad. "I'm just letting you know where I stand in case he asks."

"Are you sure you don't want to ride to the airport with us?" I asked Dad.

"I'm sure. It's better if Teddy and I stay here. We'll meet Eric when you get back. Besides, someone has to keep Jamie company," Dad said and winked at her. Jamie smiled.

"I wanna ride in the limbo," Teddy spoke up.

"No limbo for you," Mom said as she patted Teddy on the head. "You're staying home with Dad. You can greet all the newspaper reporters when they get here. Won't that be fun, Teddy?"

Mr. Starr had arranged for local newspapers to do stories about Randi's dream date. Dad had invited the reporters to our house so we'd feel comfortable talking to them.

"I wanna ride in the limbo!" Teddy announced again.

"That's limo and you can't, Teddy," Randi told him.

"Maybe the reporters will take your picture for the newspaper," I told him. "Wouldn't that be great?"

Teddy's eyes lit up. The thought of seeing himself in the newspapers seemed to make him happy. Just then, a car horn tooted.

"Da limbo is here," Teddy yelled as he raced over to the front door and jerked it open.

"Wow! Look at that car," Jamie said as she peeked out the living room window. "It's a stretch limo."

"How do I look?" Mom asked Dad. "Do I look all right?"

Dad laughed. "Who's going on this dream date anyway?"

Mom grinned and gave Dad a playful punch on the arm.

"Ouch," Dad joked as he pretended to be in pain. "And, yes, you do look beautiful. You all do. Now get out of here before the limbo leaves without you."

"Bye, Dad," Randi said as she started out the front door.

"Hey," yelled Dad. "No kiss?"

"I'll smear my lipstick," Randi told him and grinned.

"Bye, Teddy! Bye, Jamie!" I called to them.

"Bye," Teddy yelled and waved.

When we reached the limo, the driver got out. He was wearing a dark uniform and cap. He bowed and opened the back door of the car for us.

"To the airport, James," Randi joked.

"Randi," scolded Mom. "That wasn't polite."

"Sorry," Randi apologized to the driver. "I was just kidding."

"It's okay," the man replied. "I'm used to it."

"Is your name really James?" I asked.

"My name is Throckmorton," he explained. "So when people call me James, I don't mind. It's a lot easier for them to remember."

I laughed and climbed into the limo beside my mother and Randi. The driver closed the door behind me.

"Hey, Sandi! Check out this car," Randi said as she glanced around. Look at this." She pressed a button and a panel slid up. Behind it were a phone, a CD player, and a color TV.

"There's orange juice and soft drinks in the bar," the driver announced through the intercom. There was a dark glass panel that separated the front and back sections of the car.

"Thank you," Mom said, "but I think we're okay for now."

"Boy, this car is big enough to hold my whole soccer team," Randi said as the driver pulled away from the curb.

The drive to the airport was lots of fun. We watched TV, turned on the CD player, and played with all the gadgets in the car. And the neatest thing of all was the way other people watched us drive by. I felt like a famous actress.

When we got to the airport, our driver drove right by the lot we usually parked in when we picked up somebody. Instead, he turned down a special road that was marked "Private Use Only."

Mom tapped on the window that separated James's section of the car from ours. James pressed a button and the panel automatically lowered. "Yes?" James asked.

"Are we supposed to go down this road?" Mom asked.

"Yes, Mrs. Daniels," James answered. "Mr. Starr arranged everything with airport security. We'll drive right out onto the landing strip and meet Mr. Starr when he and Mr. St. John get off the plane."

"Okay," Mom said. "Thank you."

"Wow! Talk about service," Randi said as she leaned back against the leather seats. "This sure is living." She turned up the volume of the TV show she was watching. "Look at that jet," she said as we drove out on the airstrip. A private Lear jet had just landed and was taxiing toward the terminal.

"Is that Eric's plane?" I asked.

"Yes," James said as he pulled the limo over near a fence and stopped.

"Can you believe that Eric St. John is on that plane?" Randi asked as she plastered her nose against the car window.

I noticed another limousine parked nearby. "Hey, somebody else important must be on the plane, too," I said and pointed at the identical shiny car.

"I only care about seeing Eric," Randi said. "Can we get out of the car, Mom?" she asked.

"I guess so," Mom replied and turned to the driver. "Mr. Throckmorton, is it okay if we all get out of the car to wait?" she asked.

"Certainly, ma'am," James answered. He hopped out of the front and opened the back door for us. We stepped out.

"Isn't this great?" Randi yelled excitedly as the jet door opened.

"It sure is," Mom admitted.

"I can't believe this is happening," I replied.

"Look! There he is!" Randi squealed. "It's him! It's really him! It's Eric St. John!"

I turned to look at the plane. There he was, dressed in jeans and a leather jacket. Eric St. John looked just like a regular kid except for one thing. He was incredibly gorgeous! I couldn't stop myself. I started screaming as loud as Randi.

"Easy, girls," Mom said. "Don't faint. Then you'll never get to meet him."

I watched all of the people getting off of the plane with Eric. There was a tall, blond man who had to be Mr. Starr. And there was a woman with dark hair carrying a notebook in one hand. She looked like she might be an assistant or a secretary or something.

"Hi, there!" yelled Mr. Starr as he waved to us. "I'm Ken Starr. You must be the Daniels family."

"Well, we're part of it," Mom replied. "I'm Mrs. Daniels." She pointed at Randi and then me. "These are my twin daughters, Randi and Sandi."

"Hi, girls!" Mr. Starr greeted us warmly. "This is Judy Brown, my assistant. She helps to keep us all organized. And this young man here is Randi's dream date."

"I'm Eric St. John," Eric said as he took a step forward. "Hi, Randi," he said to me.

"Uh, I'm Sandi," I admitted as I blushed a deep red. "She's Randi." I pointed at my sister.

"Oh," Eric said, his eyes twinkling. "I goofed." He turned to Randi. "Hi, Randi. Glad to meet you. I'm sure we're going to have a lot of fun together."

Eric looked back and forth at us.

"Randi and Sandi," he said with a big grin. "I'll bet you confuse a lot of people. You look so much alike that you could probably switch places and nobody would ever know."

"We have," Randi blurted out. "We've pulled the old switcheroo quite a few times, haven't we, Sandi?"

Mom glared at us. I gulped and nodded. "Yeah, we have," I admitted. "And we've gotten in big trouble every time."

Eric laughed right out loud. That made us relax a little.

"Did you hear that?" Eric asked Mr. Starr.

"Yeah, and I hope we're not going to have any trouble making this video," Mr. Starr replied.

"I'm sure there won't be any trouble," Mom assured him. "Right, girls?"

"Right," I mumbled.

"Yeah, right," Randi agreed.

I glanced at Eric, and he winked. I liked him already. He sure was different than I expected him to be. Somehow I thought he'd be really stuck-up and distant. But he wasn't at all. He was warm and friendly—kind of like Randi. I wondered if he was a

fanatic about food the way Randi was.

"Why don't we get going?" Mr. Starr suggested.

"Good idea," Eric said. "I'm hungry. How about a pizza on the way?"

I grinned. Yep, he was even like Randi about food.

"Sorry, Eric, but we don't have time right now for a pizza," Mr. Starr said. "We'll have something later. Besides, didn't you just eat lunch on the plane?"

"Yeah, but it was gross," Eric said.

"Well, we have to deal with reporters first, okay?" Mr. Starr asked Eric. "I imagine they are all waiting for us at the Daniels's house."

"Okay," agreed Eric. "I can't wait to meet Teddy anyway."

"How do you know about Teddy?" I asked.

"I know about all of you," said Eric. "Your folks told Ken all about your family. And he told me about calling your house to tell you Randi had won the contest."

"Teddy's nickname is Trouble," Randi explained as we climbed into the limo. "And I'm sure you can figure out why."

Eric and Mr. Starr climbed in, too, and Throckmorton closed the door.

"Isn't Ms. Brown coming with us?" I asked.

"No, she has some other things to do," Mr. Starr explained. "She'll meet us later." I peeked out the back window and saw Mr. Starr's assistant climbing into the other limo.

"Do you know what you call a potato that looks just like another potato?" Eric asked as the limo started down the road.

"No, what?" Randi asked.

"An imi-tater," snickered Eric. We all howled at Eric's joke.

Eric told jokes and stories all the way home. He was so easy to talk to that he seemed like a good friend by the time we got to our house. I looked over at Randi and saw that she was wearing her puppy dog expression. She stared at Eric with lovesick eyes. There was the look of mush written all over her face.

There was no doubt. Randi was developing one super-sized, monstrous crush on Eric St. John.

CHAPTER Four

I wasn't ready for the chaos that was waiting for us at home. When we pulled up, a huge cheer erupted around the neighborhood.

I saw Bobbi Joy Boikin and Todd the Cod Jackson standing in the crowd.

"I'm sorry about all this," I said to Eric as Bobbi Joy pressed her face against the window and tried to peer in at us. She was weird enough, but she looked even weirder with her face smashed against the glass. "I didn't think things were going to be this crazy."

Eric laughed. "Don't be sorry," he said. "I don't mind. I'm happy that people like me enough to come out here to meet me."

"Eric is great at dealing with fans," Mr. Starr added. "He doesn't get nervous around crowds. It's amazing."

"I'm glad, but I am worried," Mom said as she looked nervously at all the kids gathered in our yard.

"That face sure scares me," Randi said as she pointed at Bobbi Joy, who was still staring through the darkened window.

"Everything will be okay," Mr. Starr assured us. "I'll go out and say something to calm them down. Then we'll let Eric say a few words and get you folks inside the house. Okay?" Without waiting for an answer, he opened the limo door and climbed out. The crowd roared.

"Hi, everyone! Thanks for coming out to say hello to Eric St. John." The kids started screaming again when they heard Eric's name. "If I could get all of you to move back from the car, Eric would like to say a few words."

Within seconds, everyone had moved back about ten feet.

"Okay," Mr. Starr said, leaning into the limo. "Throckmorton and I will stay out here with Eric. Why don't you three head into the house? It'll be easier that way."

We nodded. Mr. Starr faced the crowd. "Everyone, here's Eric St. John!"

"Well, here I go," said Eric. "Wish me luck."

The noise level really rose as Eric got out and waved to the crowd. There were shrieks and screams.

"Let's go, girls," Mom urged. She slipped out the limo door. Randi and I followed closely behind her. We weaved our way through the crowd. I turned around once and saw that Eric was signing autographs.

"That Eric is really something," Randi said as we made our way toward the house.

"He sure is," I agreed.

"Welcome home, groupies," Dad greeted us as he hurried us inside. "How do you like your reception committee?"

"I can't believe there are so many kids out there," Mom said. "Where did they all come from? And how long have they been out there?"

"I think every kid at Randi and Sandi's school must be here," Dad said. "They started lining up as soon as you left for the airport."

"Are the reporters here?" Mom asked.

Dad pointed toward the living room. "They're in there. Teddy is entertaining them."

"Entertaining them?" I asked as Randi and I walked toward the living room.

Jamie was sitting on the couch between two reporters. One was a woman and one was a man. Two photographers were sitting in chairs. And smack in the middle of everybody was Teddy, doing the wildest dance ever. His legs were going one way. His arms were flailing in the air like a sick bird. He was bouncing and spinning and turning all around. Finally, he missed a step and down he went.

"How dat?" he asked. "Was dat dance dood?"

"It was wonderful," the woman reporter said.

"It was great," added Jamie, who didn't see us behind her.

"Now, I going to do a trick," Teddy announced as

he wobbled to his feet.

"Oh, no! Not again," groaned one of the photographers. "Last time you almost broke my camera."

I decided it was time to rescue the newspaper people from Trouble.

"Teddy, Eric's outside. Why don't you go look out the window and see?" I suggested.

"He here?" Teddy's eyes grew big with excitement.

"Sure is," I said as Teddy ran toward the window.

The reporters introduced themselves to us and told us what kinds of questions they wanted to ask us. Nothing was very tough to answer. Just stuff about what we like to do, why we like being twins, and what it was like to meet Eric St. John.

A few minutes later, the front door burst open and Eric walked in with Mr. Starr.

"You must be Teddy," Eric said as he stooped to get on eye level with Teddy.

"I Teddy," he said proudly. "Are you dweeb date?"

Eric laughed, but I could tell Randi didn't think it was funny.

"It's dream date, not dweeb date, Teddy," Randi scolded him.

"It's okay," Eric said as he shook Teddy's hand. "When I was little, I couldn't figure out how to say meatloaf. I said meatlump. It drove my mom crazy for a long time."

"Can I quote you on that?" asked a reporter as the photographers took shots of Eric and Teddy shaking hands.

"Sure," Eric agreed.

The reporters fired off questions for the next ten minutes. Eric answered casually and politely. Nothing seemed to upset him or make him nervous.

"Well, I think that's enough questions for today, gang," Mr. Starr announced. "You'll get another chance to talk to Eric at the soccer game tomorrow."

The reporters and photographers nodded and stood up to leave. Dad led them to the front door.

"Come on, Jamie," I said. I led her toward Eric, who was standing between Randi and Teddy. "Eric, this is my best friend, Jamie Collins."

"I love the way you sing," Jamie said.

"Thanks, Jamie," said Eric. "That's a nice thing to say. I'm pleased to meet you." Eric smiled a perfect smile. "Are there only pretty girls in this town?"

Jamie blushed and giggled.

"I guess you didn't see Bobbi Joy Boikin," Randi said with a devilish grin.

"You can point her out to me," Eric said and grinned.

"Eric, I think we should get going," Mr. Starr said as he joined our group. "We have a lot to do before tomorrow."

"Right," Eric replied. "Tomorrow is a busy day. There's the soccer game, lunch, and rehearsing for the video."

"I can't wait," Randi said. "So what are we having for lunch?"

That was a real Randi Daniels question. She was more concerned with lunch than the soccer game or the video. No matter what happened in her life, Randi's stomach came first.

"You can have anything you want," Eric said. "I know what I won't be having."

"What?" asked Jamie.

"Meatlump," joked Eric. "I hate meatlump." We all laughed.

"What's your favorite food?" I asked him.

"I like yum-yum-yummy Super Pops!" shouted Teddy before Eric had a chance to answer.

"That's Teddy's favorite cereal," Randi explained.

"My favorite food is kind of weird," Eric said to make us curious.

"What is it?" Randi asked.

"You won't believe it. I love liver and onions," Eric said.

I made a sick face. So did Jamie.

"Liver and onions are good," Randi mumbled. "I like it, too."

"You hate it," I said to my sister. "Tell the truth."

"Well, it's not my favorite," Randi said. "But it's not that bad."

"For some reason, I love it," Eric said. "So if the restaurant has it tomorrow, that's what I'll get. You could even do me a big favor. If I'm late to lunch for some reason, could you order liver for

52

me? It'd save some time."

"Sure," Randi agreed.

"Throckmorton is waiting for us, Eric," Mr. Starr said. "Let's go to the hotel and get settled."

"Bye," Eric said. "See you tomorrow."

"Bye!" called Randi.

Dad opened the front door. Mr. Starr and Eric started down the walk toward the limo. A few kids were still hanging around outside. They rushed up to get Eric's autograph.

"He's a nice boy," Dad said as we watched them leave.

"And cute," Randi added.

"He sure is!" Jamie agreed.

"He has a nice sense of humor," Mom added.

"But he has weird taste in food," I said. "Liver and onions. Yuck!"

"Eric da dweeb date," Teddy said loudly as he headed upstairs. "Hoppy want to meet him."

That was one thing we didn't need. Teddy and Hoppy together always meant trouble. Eric had better watch out.

CHAPTER Five

BY the time we got to the soccer field the next morning, the place was mobbed. Police officers were trying to keep the crowd under control. There were little kids running around and screaming. And tons of parents were standing around and watching the whole crazy scene.

As Dad searched for a place to park, I noticed two video production vans parked near Eric's limo.

Members of our rec soccer team were kicking the ball around the field. Coach Matthews and Ms. Morgan from the recreation commission were watching them from the sidelines.

"This place is a circus," Dad complained.

"Do you see Eric anywhere?" Randi asked.

"Nope," I said as I adjusted my glasses. I never wore my contacts while playing soccer or other sports. I didn't want to take the chance of losing them.

"I don't either," Jamie added.

"Well, I see a police officer," Mom interrupted. "And it looks as if he wants to tell us something."

Dad stopped the car and the police officer leaned down to talk to him.

"Sir, the lot is filled. The soccer field is closed to the public today," the officer said sternly.

"I know, but we have to be here," Dad told him. "We're the Daniels family."

The officer's face brightened. "You are? Which one of you girls won the contest?"

"She did," I said, pointing at my sister.

"Congratulations!" the officer said to Randi. "It's certainly brought some excitement to our town."

"Thanks," Randi replied.

"So where should I park?" Dad asked.

"Just follow me. You can park near the limo," the officer said.

After speaking to several other officials, the officer cleared a path through the crowd so Dad could park the car.

"Look!" Jamie cried, pointing to Bobbi Joy Boikin.

"Why does she have to be here?" Randi grumbled as she waved to Bobbi Joy through the window.

"I wanta go home," Teddy grumbled.

"Why is Teddy in such a bad mood?" Jamie asked.

"He's mad because Dad wouldn't let him bring his dumb frog with him," Randi explained.

"Hoppy not dumb," Trouble muttered.

"A frog doesn't belong in the car or at a soccer game," Dad said from the front seat.

"Maybe we should have let Teddy bring Hoppy," Mom said. "At least he'd have something to keep him busy."

"You know the way Hoppy jumps around. He probably would've gotten lost," Dad said. "Okay, everybody out."

We all jumped out and headed toward the limo.

"Hi, James!" Randi yelled to the limo driver.

"Hi, girls," he said and smiled at us.

"This is Jamie Collins," Randi said. "Jamie, meet James."

"His name is really Throckmorton," I said.

"I like James better," Jamie said.

"So do I," James replied.

Ms. Brown walked up just as Mom and Dad caught up with us. "Good morning," she greeted us.

"Good morning," Dad replied. "How are things going?"

"Great," Ms. Brown said. "The video crew is ready. The team looks warmed up and ready. So I'm glad you're all here. Do you need a few minutes to practice?"

"Maybe just a second, but I think we're ready," I said, glancing at Randi. I saw that she was scanning the crowd, probably for a glimpse of Eric.

"Ms. Brown, this is our friend Jamie," I said.

"Nice to meet you," she told Jamie.

"Where's Mr. Starr?" Mom asked.

Ms. Brown grinned. "He's prowling through the

crowd looking for interesting faces. He wants to pick five or six other kids to be in the game, too."

"Where's Eric?" Randi blurted out.

"In the limo," Ms. Brown answered.

"Can we talk to him?" Randi asked.

"Sure," Ms. Brown said. "When we're ready to start taping, we'll call you."

"Come on," Randi said to Jamie and me.

We went up to the limo and tapped on the dark glass. The window lowered and we saw Eric sitting in the backseat all alone.

"Hi, Eric!" I said. "How are you?"

"Okay," Eric replied meekly. "How are you?"

"We're great!" Randi answered for me. "Can we get in the limo with you? We could talk for a while before the game starts."

"Sure," Eric answered softly.

We climbed inside and closed the door. For a few seconds, we all sat silently in the back of the limo. Eric seemed really nervous around us. Finally, I couldn't stand the quiet.

"Do you notice anything different about me

today?" I asked Eric.

He stared blankly at me. Then he slowly shook his head.

"I'm wearing my glasses today," I explained. "Yesterday I had my contacts in."

"Oh, sure, Randi," Eric said.

"I'm Sandi," I corrected him.

"I'm Randi," my sister said. "Eric, tell Jamie that joke you told us yesterday about the potato."

Eric fidgeted in his seat. "Potato?"

"You know," Randi prodded. "The joke about the two potatoes."

Eric shrugged. "Sorry. I guess I don't remember it."

"You don't remember what you call a potato that looks just like another potato?" Randi asked.

"Uh, an imi-tater?" he asked.

"Right!" Randi encouraged him. Jamie giggled. I didn't. *Why was Eric guessing at the answer to his own joke?*

"Let's go kick a ball around until they're ready for us," Randi suggested.

59

"You go ahead," Eric said as Randi reached for the door handle. "I'll wait here."

"Why?" Randi asked as she opened the door.

"There are too many people out there," Eric confessed.

"So?" Randi asked.

"So it makes me uncomfortable," Eric admitted.

"You're kidding, right?" Randi asked. "You sure weren't uncomfortable yesterday."

"That was yesterday," said Eric. "Go ahead without me. I'll come out when the game starts."

We all jumped out and headed onto the field.

"Boy, Eric sure is acting weird," Jamie spoke up. "He was lots friendlier before."

Just then a soccer ball came rolling at us. Randi trapped the ball with her foot, then booted it back to Billy Parker.

"Thanks, Randi," Billy said. "I can't wait to get started. This is going to be a blast."

"Yeah," Randi said.

"I'm dying to meet Eric St. John," said Sylvia Rumsford as she joined our group. "What's he like?"

"He's nice, but kind of strange," Jamie said.

"Strange?" Sylvia asked.

"Yeah, one minute he loves getting a lot of attention and the next he doesn't," I explained. "That's why he's hiding out in the limo until the game starts."

"Maybe he just likes privacy," said Chris Miles as he came up dribbling a soccer ball.

A whistle blew from the sidelines. I turned and saw that Ms. Brown was waving her arms to get our attention.

"Will the soccer players come over here, please?" Ms. Brown called. "Mr. Starr wants to get started."

We walked over to where Ms. Brown was standing.

"Hello, everyone," Mr. Starr said. "And a special good morning to Randi and Sandi Daniels."

He looked at us and smiled. All the kids clapped. I was embarrassed, but Randi loved it.

"Now we're going to play a staged soccer game," Mr. Starr announced. "The idea is to make Eric St. John and Randi Daniels look good. We want

them to handle the ball a lot and to score goals."
Mr. Starr looked at the crowd of kids gathered
before him. "I know you're all used to playing hard
and going for the win. But just this once, I'd appreciate your help in letting Randi and Eric be the
star players. Where are those kids I picked out
earlier?"

"Here they are," Ms. Brown said as she ushered
five other kids onto the field.

"I don't believe it," Randy muttered.

Bobbi Joy Boikin and Todd the Cod Jackson
were two of the kids. I glared at them as Mr. Starr
explained to everyone exactly how we were supposed to move down the field and who would score
when.

"Okay," he called out. "Eric will join us now."

The crowd cheered as Eric climbed out of the
limo and walked toward us. Girls shrieked. Eric
looked super-embarrassed by the whole thing.

"Everyone get into position," Mr. Starr shouted.

"Good luck," Mom called to us from the sidelines. I saw Mom, Dad, and Trouble standing with

our teacher, Ms. Morgan, and Coach Matthews. I waved.

"You're going to get it," someone whispered. I turned and saw Bobbi Joy talking to Randi. "I'll fix you for not picking me to be in your crummy video," Bobbi Joy threatened as she walked past Randi.

I walked over to Randi. "Do you want me to tell Mr. Starr?"

Randi smiled. "No, I'll just ignore her."

"Could we have Randi and Eric in the middle of the field, please?" Mr. Starr shouted. He held a soccer ball in one hand.

Mr. Starr put the ball on the ground. "In our first scene, the ball gets passed to Eric. He dribbles down the field, then he shoots and scores. Everyone knows what to do, so let's do it!"

He quickly moved out of view of the cameras. The whistle sounded to signal the beginning of play. Randi kicked the ball to Chris Miles. He dribbled and passed to Eric, who was running down the sideline. He quickly took the ball and dribbled with ease toward the goal. He faked out Billy Parker and went right for the goalie, Todd the Cod. He fired a wicked shot that zipped past Todd and into the net for a score.

Randi and I raced up to Eric. "You're a great player," I said.

"Yeah, that was a terrific shot," Randi said.

"Thanks," said Eric shyly. His green eyes twinkled as he looked at us. "I love soccer. I was the leading scorer on my school team three years in a row."

Ms. Brown blew her whistle. "Okay. Now it's Randi's turn to score. Back in your places everyone."

"Good luck, Randi," said Eric as we jogged back up the field.

We got in position and the cameras started rolling. Jamie kicked the ball to me. I passed the ball to Randi. Randi dribbled around Sylvia Rumsford and headed for the goal. But before Randi could get a clean shot, Bobbi Joy stepped in front of her and stuck out her foot. Blam! Randi tripped and fell.

Ms. Brown blew the whistle.

"Hey!" yelled Eric as he rushed over and helped Randi to her feet. He pointed at Bobbi Joy. "You did that on purpose."

"I did not," Bobbi Joy said. "It was an accident."

"No, it wasn't!" I yelled as I ran up to her.

"Bobbi Joy stuck her foot out on purpose," Jamie said.

"Let's give it another shot," Mr. Starr said. "And, Bobbi Joy, I'll have my eye on you next time, so please watch where your feet are. If you do try to trip Randi or keep her from scoring, you're off the field."

The next take went perfectly. Randi dribbled in and out and got a clean shot right into the goal.

"Cut!" yelled Mr. Starr. "That was great!"

"You did it!" I yelled, running up to Randi.

"Yeah, nice going," Eric said.

"That's all for today," Mr. Starr announced. "I thank all of you for coming out here and being part of Randi Daniels's special dream date. We'll meet you girls later for lunch. And remember, we're

going to rehearse the music video right after we eat."

Randi and I nodded.

"Well, bye," Eric said. "I'd better get out of here before I get mobbed."

I watched as he headed toward his waiting limo.

"I still can't figure him out," I said to Randi. "He seems like two different people."

"Well, if he is, both of them are gorgeous," Randi sighed.

"I hungee," Teddy exclaimed suddenly. "I hungee. Want Yum-Yum-Yummy Super Pops!"

"I hungee, too," I said. "Let's hurry and change for lunch."

"Yeah," Randi agreed as she watched Eric's limo drive off. "Let's hurry."

CHAPTER **Six**

"I wonder why Mr. Starr and Eric are so late," Dad said as we sat down at our table. We were having lunch at the fanciest restaurant in town.

"Maybe Eric was tired," Mom said. "Besides, the twins dressed so fast I think they set a new record."

"I hungee," Teddy announced so loudly that people at the tables around us laughed.

It was embarrassing. I wished I could have turned invisible.

"I hungee," Teddy repeated even louder. I sunk down in my chair and tried to bury my face in the menu. I didn't want anyone to see that my cheeks were turning pink. I wanted to stand up and tell everyone that Teddy had followed us into the restaurant and that we really didn't know him.

"I hungee! I hungee! I hungee!" Teddy complained.

"Be quiet, Trouble!" Randi said sternly. "You'll have something to eat in a few minutes."

"I hungee now!" Teddy exclaimed. I think he even embarassed the waiter. He rushed over to our table and asked to take our order.

"Would you like a little something now before Eric St. John arrives?" the waiter asked, glancing right at Teddy.

"Maybe we should," Mom suggested. "I'm sure Mr. Starr won't mind."

"Yeah, Eric said to go ahead and order for him," Randi spoke up.

"He did?" Dad asked in surprise.

"Yeah, he wants liver and onions," I told him. I saw the waiter jot that down on his pad of paper.

Randi and I ordered the roast beef dinner. Mom and Dad both chose the chicken breast dinner. And Dad ordered a cheeseburger with French fries for Teddy.

"Yum-Yum-Yummy Super Pops!" Teddy said.

"No, Teddy," Mom said. "You had Super Pops cereal for breakfast. You're having a cheeseburger now."

"Thank you," the waiter said, looking at my little brother like he was a monster. He collected the menus and left.

"Are you sure Eric wanted liver and onions for lunch?" Dad asked. "Maybe we should've waited for him to get here."

"He told us to order, Dad. Honest," I said.

"Yeah, he said he loved liver," Randi agreed.

"Well, okay," Dad said.

"I hungee," Teddy whined.

"The food is on the way," Mom promised Teddy.

"I sure hope the food gets here fast. That little fellow sounds starved." I turned around to see Mr. Starr and Eric approaching our table. "We knew we were in the right place when we heard Teddy. Sorry we're late," Mr. Starr said.

"Hi, Eric," Randi said.

"Hello again," Eric said as he and Mr. Starr sat down. Eric looked at me. "I see you're not wearing your glasses now," he said.

"I like my contacts better," I explained.

"We went ahead and ordered," Mom said. "I hope you don't mind, but Teddy was getting fussy."

"No problem," said Mr. Starr.

"I hungee," Teddy repeated for the hundredth time. This time he used his cute, soft voice that was hard to resist. Everyone chuckled.

"I hungee, too," Eric whispered to Teddy.

Mr. Starr signaled to the waiter. "Eric, what looks good to you?" he asked, scanning the menu.

"We already ordered Eric's lunch," Randi interrupted. "He asked us to."

"I did?" Eric mumbled. He gave Randi a strange look.

"Yeah, after your meatlump story yesterday, you asked us to order your favorite food for you if you were late," I said, trying to refresh Eric's memory.

"Oh, sure," Eric said. He grinned weakly.

Mr. Starr ordered and the waiter left.

"Are you girls ready for rehearsal today?" Mr. Starr asked. "It should be a lot of fun."

71

"I can't wait," I admitted.

"We rented a dancing school's facilities for the day so we could get the camera angles right. Eric and the band need to do some practicing, too," Mr. Starr explained.

"Where's the band?" Randi asked eagerly.

"They're getting settled in," Mr. Starr explained. "Their plane just arrived from the coast. A new singer named Melanie, who has a small part in the video, should be arriving soon, too. I hope she gets to rehearsal on time."

"So what will Sandi and I be doing at rehearsal?" Randi asked.

"We'll walk you through your parts for the video," Mr. Starr said. "Today's rehearsal will be pretty quiet. No crowd. It'll just be you two, Eric and his band, and Melanie. We'll have a full rehearsal with all the kids tomorrow before the taping."

"Why the closed rehearsal?" Mom asked.

"Eric decided he'd feel more comfortable that way," Mr. Starr explained. "This is his very first live video, so it's important that he gets all the kinks out before he gets in front of a crowd. But you're both welcome to come and watch. Teddy, too."

"I hungee," Teddy said.

Just then, the waiter brought our orders to the table. Teddy dug right in.

Eric's eyes almost bulged out of his head when he saw what was on his plate. He gulped and turned a strange shade of white.

"Let's eat," Dad said. "I think we're all starved."

Everyone started to eat except Eric. He stared at the liver and onions, then picked up his fork and knife and poked at his food like he was trying to push it off his plate.

"No hungee?" Teddy asked Eric.

Before Eric could answer, Teddy oozed ketchup off his plate and all over his lap.

"Oh, Teddy!" said Mom as she dabbed at the red blobs with a napkin.

"Why aren't you eating?" Randi asked Eric as she sliced her roast beef. "I thought you were starved."

"I was," Eric said. "But now I don't think I feel too well."

"But liver and onions is your favorite," I said. "Don't you want it?"

"Yes, it's fine," Eric assured us.

Eric sliced off a little piece. He stuck his fork in it and lifted it to his mouth. He chewed and chewed. It was almost like he didn't want to swallow it. Finally, there was a loud gulp.

"Is the liver pretty bad?" I asked him.

"Yeah, I guess I only like California liver," Eric explained quickly. He pushed his plate away. "Besides, I have to sing this afternoon and I sing better on an empty stomach."

"My tomach not empty," bragged Teddy. "I full." He tapped his tummy with his hand and burped the loudest burp I ever heard. Everyone laughed except me and Randi.

"That was a good lunch," Mr. Starr said. "And we know that Teddy enjoyed it." He smiled at Teddy. "Now it's time for rehearsal. Do you want to drive the girls over or should I?" he asked Mom and Dad.

"I think we'd better take Teddy home and change his clothes," Mom said.

"If it's okay, we'll let the girls ride over with you," Dad said. "Then we'll pick them up later."

"Or I could have Throckmorton take them home afterward," Mr. Starr offered.

"Awesome," Randi said. "Can he drop us off at the rec center, Mom? It's Saturday and everyone will be there. It'd be so cool to ride up in a limo."

"Sure, it's okay," Mom agreed.

"Otay!" echoed Teddy. Then he started to hiccup. Mom gave him some water. Teddy took a sip, but the hiccups wouldn't stop.

By the time the waiter cleared away the dishes and took Mr. Starr's money, Teddy's hiccups sounded like a machine gun. Everyone in the restaurant was staring at us again. Randi and I practically ran out the front door to get away from him.

Lunch had been a disaster! What else could possibly go wrong during this dream date?

CHAPTER **Seven**

RANDI and I hopped in the limo beside Eric. I waved to Mom and Dad as their car pulled away from the curb.

"What's the backup singer like?" Randi asked Eric.

"Melanie's really talented," he said. "I think we're lucky to have her in the video with us."

Randi badgered Eric with all kinds of questions until we pulled up in front of the dance school.

"Everybody out," Eric announced. He seemed happy that Randi's interview with him was over.

"Go right on inside, girls," James said cheerfully. "Have a good time."

As we stepped through the doors, rock-and-roll

music blared at us. It sounded great. Randi suddenly stopped, turned around to look at me, and grinned from ear to ear.

"This is going to be totally outrageous," she said. "I can't believe this is really happening to us."

"Yeah, it's awesome," I agreed as we followed Eric into a large room filled with people and music.

The band was set up on risers near the back of the room. There was a microphone stand in front of the band. I couldn't wait to hear Eric sing.

"Boy, I love show business already," Randi said.

I nodded as I watched people bustling around the room. "There's Ms. Brown," I said, pointing. She was talking to Mr. Starr. They both looked worried about something. "Let's go see what's going on."

"I can't believe this is happening!" Mr. Starr complained as we walked toward them. "Can't you find a replacement for her?"

"Not this late," Ms. Brown said. "And even if we could track somebody down to fill in, there's no time to get them here and go through a rehearsal."

Then she saw us standing there. "Hi, girls,"

she said cheerfully.

"What's wrong?" I asked.

"A lot," Mr. Starr said.

"Yeah, the backup singer, Melanie, can't make it," said a guy with a bushy beard. "She lost her voice. Her part was pretty small, but the song needs a female singer. So we might have to postpone the whole thing and do it back in California. By the way, I'm Marty. I'm producing this video."

"Nice to meet you," I said, noticing how disappointed Randi looked. "Isn't there anything we can do to help?"

"Do you know a girl who could sing Melanie's part?" Mr. Starr asked.

Randi looked at me and grinned. I knew that look all too well. I knew exactly what she was thinking.

I looked deep into her eyes and shook my head. There was no way that Randi Daniels was going to do this to me again. No way.

"Is it a complicated part?" Randi asked Mr. Starr.

"Not really," said Ms. Brown. "The main problem is we'd need her to get here pretty quick and run through a rehearsal with us."

"I know someone who could do it. She sings really well," Randi said before I could stop her.

"Really?" Eric asked as he joined our group.

Randi nodded.

"Who?" he asked.

"Me!" Randi said proudly, even though she knew she couldn't sing a single note.

I knew Randi was counting on me to bail her out—again. I didn't want to be a part of it. We'd promised Mom and Dad that we'd never secretly switch places again. And I planned to stick to my promise.

I tried to motion to her with my eyes to shut up. She ignored me and went on and on about how excited she was to help.

"Your sister is great," Eric said to me. "She's solved everything for us."

"Yeah, she sure has," I grumbled sarcastically. "I bet you can't imagine what it's like to have a twin."

"I think I can," Eric mumbled.

I wondered what he was talking about. You

couldn't know what it was like to be a twin unless you had one.

"How about singing for us right now?" Mr. Starr asked.

"I-I can't," Randi sputtered. "I have to go to the restroom first. Where is it?"

"Let me show you," Ms. Brown offered.

"Let's go, Sandi," Randi said as she practically dragged me with her.

"We'll be ready for you when you get back," Mr. Starr called after us.

Randi and I followed Ms. Brown down the hall. "There it is," Ms. Brown said.

"Thanks," Randi said and pulled me through the door with her.

"Okay? What's the big idea?" I asked angrily. "You can't sing and you know it."

"I'm not going to sing," Randi said, grinning at me. "You are."

"I don't want to sing," I snapped. "And I'm not going to."

"But we have to save the video, Sandi," Randi

pleaded. "The video is part of my prize and I won't get to do it without your help. Eric and Mr. Starr will go back to California and film the whole thing there. And all the kids will be mad at me."

Randi really did look upset. She looked like she might cry at any second.

"We promised Mom and Dad that we wouldn't pull the old switcheroo again," I reminded her. "Remember?"

"We'll figure something out, Sandi," Randi assured me. "Please! Just one last time. Please help me."

"Every time we switch places we end up in big trouble," I reminded Randi.

"Those other times were different," Randi argued. "What trouble can we get into this time?"

Just then, there was a knock at the door. "Are you almost ready?" Ms. Brown called through the door. "Everyone is waiting."

"I'll be right there," Randi answered. She looked at me with pleading puppy-dog eyes. "Please, Sandi? This video means a lot to me. I'd do it for you."

I couldn't stand to see her beg. "Okay, okay," I said. "Let's hurry and change clothes."

"Oh, Sandi! Thanks!" Randi exclaimed as we began the switch.

We quickly swapped clothes. Luckily we both had the same hairstyle. And it was a good thing I'd worn my contacts or I would have had to take off my glasses and feel my way around the room.

"Ready?" Randi asked as we checked ourselves in the mirror.

"Ready," I answered. Arm in arm we went into the hall. Ms. Brown was waiting for us.

"Good! I thought maybe you had a case of stage fright," Ms. Brown said. She rushed us back into the rehearsal room.

"Okay, Randi," said Mr. Starr when he saw me. "Go stand near Eric. We've set up a microphone for you."

"Give it your best shot, San . . . Randi," my sister called as I took my place on the riser next to Eric.

"This is Randi Daniels," Mr. Starr said to the band. "She's going to sing Melanie's part." I looked at the band members. They smiled and nodded to me.

Marty handed me a sheet with music and lyrics on it. He gave me a few quick instructions. It seemed easy enough.

"Try it once without music," he suggested.

"Just relax and do your best," Mr. Starr said.

"You can do it," Eric said.

"Knock their socks off, Randi," Randi called to me.

I checked the music sheet once more, then looked up and sang my heart out. I didn't think. I just sang. When I stopped, the room was completely silent. It was so quiet that it scared me. Then everyone started clapping.

"That was super!" Mr. Starr said.

"We found our singer," Marty agreed.

"Very nice," Ms. Brown said.

"You're great, Randi," Eric said.

"Thank you," I said as I felt my cheeks turning pink.

"Let's do it with music," Mr. Starr shouted.

"Okay," Marty said, turning to Eric and me. "I'm

going out to the truck to work on the camera takes. I'll talk to you through Ms. Brown. We have a portable intercom system."

"I'll be outside in the truck, too," Mr. Starr said as he followed Marty out of the room. Ms. Brown put on a headset so she could hear what they were saying to her.

I looked at Randi. She crossed her fingers for me.

"Quiet, everyone," Ms. Brown announced. The room fell silent. "Get ready on stage. We'll start in ten seconds, Eric."

Eric nodded. He looked at me and winked.

"Okay, five, four, three . . ." Ms. Brown counted down until she pointed at Eric to start.

I couldn't help but sway in time to the music. When my part came I belted out the words. I sang out as loud and strong as I could. As my words faded out, Eric picked up the lyrics and kept going. It was beautiful. Our voices blended so well together. The whole experience was like a magical dream.

When we finished, the camera people, the technicians, and Randi cheered.

"The word from the big guys in the van is that it's perfect," Ms. Brown said. "You two don't need any more rehearsing. Just do it like that tomorrow."

"Uh, yeah, tomorrow," Eric said glumly.

"Eric, go ahead and try out your love song for fun," Ms. Brown suggested. "I'm sure Randi and Sandi would love to hear you sing it."

"Yeah," Randi agreed.

"Your voice is wonderful, Eric," I said as I walked past him and hopped off the risers.

"Thanks," he said.

"I was great," Randi whispered to me and giggled.

The band began to play. This time the music was soft and sweet. Eric sang a very romantic song. I could tell Randi loved it. She had that puppy-dog look on her face again.

In the middle of the song, Eric stopped singing. Then the band stopped playing.

"I can't do it," Eric said. "I just can't do it."

He put down his microphone and hopped off the risers. He walked toward the exit. Ms. Brown chased after him.

"Eric, what's wrong?" I asked as I caught up to him.

He stopped and looked at Randi and me. "Everything is wrong," he said.

"Like what?" I asked him. "Tell us. Maybe we can help."

"I'll never be able to do that live concert tomorrow in front of all those kids. We'll have to cancel the video."

"But why?" Randi blurted out.

"You don't understand," Eric groaned. "Recording songs in a studio is easy. You don't have to get up in front of all those people. I've never done a live show and it scares me to death."

"Eric, relax," Ms. Brown said as she joined us.

"I can't do it," Eric told her. "There's no way."

Just then, Mr. Starr flew into the room. "Eric! What's wrong?" he asked.

"You know what's wrong," Eric muttered. "I'm scared. I'm nervous. I can't get up there tomorrow in front of all those kids."

I looked at Randi. She looked at me. What

was going on? Eric St. John was a star. Why was he so scared about singing in front of people?

Eric turned toward us. "You think I'm crazy, don't you?" he asked.

"No," I said. "But we don't understand what's going on."

"Since you're twins, maybe you'll understand," Eric said.

"No, Eric," said Mr. Starr.

"Don't," Ms. Brown warned.

"I think they deserve to know what's going on," Eric said. "I think Randi and Sandi are great. They can be trusted with our secret."

"Okay," Mr. Starr agreed, "but you girls must promise never to share this secret with anyone."

"We promise," we said together.

"Okay," Eric said. "Come with us. You're not going to believe this."

CHAPTER Eight

WE headed toward the big truck in the parking lot. I was surprised when Eric passed the van, kept walking, and pulled open the door on a big R.V. sitting near the edge of the lot.

"Remember your promise, girls," Mr. Starr said from behind us.

We both nodded and followed Eric into the vehicle.

I couldn't believe my eyes. I felt like I had double vision. Right in front of us sat a second Eric St. John. But how could there be two Erics?

Then, strangely, it all made sense. The Erics were twins—just like Randi and me.

"I can't believe it," I sputtered.

"What are they doing here?" the second Eric asked nervously.

"I decided they should know our secret," the first Eric said. "Especially since I've decided that I can't do it tomorrow. I'll freeze right on stage. I know it."

"Eric, quit panicking," his brother said. "We'll figure it out somehow."

I looked at Randi. She hadn't said a word.

"You're twins," I said. "I just can't believe it."

"Yep, identical twins," Mr. Starr said. "Randi and Sandi, meet Eric and Derrick St. John. Well, actually you've met them both already."

"We have?" Randi asked. "Did we meet Derrick at the airport?"

Derrick grinned. "Yeah, that was me," he confessed.

"We wondered why you changed so much," I told him. "You loved the crowd at our house and then you didn't at the soccer game. It all makes sense now."

"Yeah, Eric played soccer because he's a lot better at sports than I am," Derrick explained.

"So who was at lunch?" Randi asked.

"I was," Eric said. "And that was a rotten trick that Derrick played on me. He knows that I hate liver and onions."

I couldn't help it. I started giggling. The whole scene was too much like something Randi and I would do to trick each other.

Derrick started laughing, too. "Yeah, I only wished I could've been at lunch to see his face when the waiter gave him liver."

"Believe me, he looked sick," I told Derrick. "I think he managed to get down one bite before he said he liked California liver better."

"We've been switcherooed," Randi said. "Us! The masters of switcheroo have been fooled."

"But why do you guys switch places?" I asked.

"Sit down, girls," Mr. Starr said. "We'll explain."

As I sat down, I glanced at my clothes and remembered we were playing switcheroo ourselves. The whole thing was too crazy.

"Eric has a great singing voice," Mr. Starr said. "He can sing up a storm, but he's afraid to perform in front of a crowd. I guess you could call it stage fright. He may get over it in time, but for now he's scared to death. We were hoping that once he rehearsed today, he'd feel more relaxed about it."

"And Derrick is great with crowds and autographs and stuff like that," Ms. Brown explained. "He doesn't mind all the attention. But he doesn't sing as well as Eric does."

"So when Eric has to do interviews or meet a group of fans, I do it for him," Derrick said.

"I'm sure you two can understand this better than most people would," Eric said.

I fidgeted a little, knowing we were lying to them, too.

"Yeah, we can," I said honestly, glancing at Randi. "But how did you record all those songs if you have stage fright?"

Eric grinned and shrugged his shoulders. "It's easy," he said. "I've recorded all my songs in a studio. It's a lot of fun. But after you start to become famous, everyone wants you to do live concerts and stuff. I guess I hadn't thought about doing all that. I just wanted to sing my songs."

"And videos are so hot right now," Mr. Starr added. "Eric really needs to get a video of his newest song out there for people to see."

"And I thought I'd be able to do it," Eric said, looking down at the table. "But when I get in front of a crowd, I know I'll faint or forget all the words."

"We knew this switcheroo stuff could catch up with us," Derrick admitted. "But it seemed like the only way."

"Yeah, we know what you mean. Right, Randi?" I asked.

"I thought you were Randi," Ms. Brown said.

I looked at my twin sister, then at Mr. Starr.

"Now we have a confession to make," I said. "I'm not Randi. I'm Sandi."

Derrick and Eric looked back and forth between us.

"What?" Mr. Starr asked. "Not you, too."

"Yep. Randi can't sing, but she offered to fill in for Melanie," I explained.

Randi nodded. "I convinced Sandi to pretend to

be me and sing so we could save the video," she added. "Sandi has the singing talent in our family."

Derrick looked at Eric. Ms. Brown and Mr. Starr exchanged weird glances. I thought they might yell or something. Instead, they all burst out laughing.

"This is the most bizarre mess I've ever been in," Mr. Starr said.

"At least we know who everybody is now," Ms. Brown said. "I feel left out though. I don't have a twin to switch places with."

"So who has a bright idea about what to do tomorrow?" Eric asked.

No one said anything.

"Well, whatever happens," Eric said. "I want you both to know that I've enjoyed the trip here to meet you."

"That goes double for me," Derrick chimed in. "And I'm glad you know our secret. It makes it a little easier to know that you understand what's going on."

"And we won't tell anyone," I assured them.

"Yeah, but I guess we'd better get going," Randi

said. "Our friends are waiting for us at the rec center."

"I hate to let your friends down tomorrow," Mr. Starr said. "I hope we can think of something." He looked at Ms. Brown. "Please ask Throckmorton to drive the girls to the rec center."

Ms. Brown nodded. We followed her out of the R.V.

"Bye, Eric! Bye, Derrick!" I called to them.

"Bye, Sandi! Bye, Randi," they replied together.

As we walked toward the limo, I couldn't help but think about tomorrow. I wished that I could come up with a way to save the video. But how?

CHAPTER **Nine**

"THANKS for the ride, James," Randi said as we stepped out of the limo.

"Yeah, thanks," I echoed.

"See you tomorrow, girls," James said.

He got back in the car and drove away.

"You sure were quiet during the ride over," Randi said. "Why are you so upset about the video? I'm the one who won the contest."

"I'm not upset," I told her. "I was trying to figure out a way to help Eric and Derrick. I really like them."

"Me, too," Randi said. "But there's nothing we can do. There's only one Eric. If he won't get up on stage, there's no way around it."

"You're right," I said as the door to the rec center

flew open. Jamie Collins and Sylvia Rumsford ran toward us.

"Wow! You got to ride here in a limo!" Jamie gushed.

"How cool!" Sylvia said.

"How was rehearsal?" Jamie asked as we walked inside.

"Very interesting," I told her.

There was music piped throughout the rec center. But it wasn't half as cool as listening to a live band.

"It was great," Randi said. "Eric's band is the best."

"Boy, you two are the luckiest girls in the whole world," Sylvia squealed.

The other kids heard Sylvia shriek and ran to gather around us.

"Did Eric sing?" one boy asked.

"Yeah," I replied. "And he sounds even better in person."

"Are the guys in his band cute, too?" a girl asked.

"I didn't notice," Randi said. "I was too busy watching Eric."

"Didn't you find out any secrets?" Sylvia asked.

I gulped when I heard that question. We had found out the biggest secret in the whole world, but it was going to stay a secret.

"No, there's nothing juicy to tell," I said.

"I have a question," Jamie said.

"What?" Randi asked.

"Why are you wearing each other's clothes?" she asked.

We'd forgotten all about switching our clothes back. And Jamie knew us so well that she could easily tell us apart.

"It's a long story," I said. "I'll tell you about it while we're changing. Let's go."

"You will?" Randi sputtered as she rolled her eyes at me.

"Of course," I said. "Jamie can be trusted. She's our best friend. I'm going to tell her how we switched places at rehearsal and how I sang with Eric."

Randi sighed with relief that I wasn't going to tell Jamie about Eric and Derrick.

"You sang with Eric?" Jamie exclaimed. "That's so romantic!"

"Yeah, it was pretty neat," I admitted as we headed into the rest room. While Randi and I changed, we told Jamie all about Melanie's laryngitis and how Randi jumped in to save the day.

"Are you going to tell your parents about the switcheroo?" Jamie asked.

"No way," I said. "Besides, I've decided that I'm not going to do the video. We promised Mom and Dad last time that we wouldn't switch again. And Randi won the contest. It wouldn't be right for me to be in the video."

What did it matter anyway? I wondered. *There probably wouldn't even be a video to worry about.*

"You won't do it?" Randi asked, looking horrified.

"Let's worry about it tomorrow, okay?" I asked her. "Right now we have other things to worry about."

"Yeah, like me," a familiar voice said. We all stopped dead in our tracks.

"Hello, Bobbi Joy," Randi said.

Bobbi Joy made a sour face and stepped toward Randi. She looked mad.

"You know, I could've ruined your whole soccer

game if I'd wanted to," she said.

"Now, why would you have wanted to do that?" I asked sweetly to make her even madder.

"Because I should've been the one to win that contest, not you," Bobbi Joy growled.

"You entered the contest, too?" Randi asked with a grin. "I didn't know that."

"How'd you like a knuckle sandwich, Daniels?" Bobbi Joy grumbled.

"No, thanks," Randi said. "I won, so there's nothing for me to fight about."

"Girls! That's enough talk about fighting," Ms. Morgan said as she walked up behind us. She usually worked at the rec center on Saturdays. "You know the rec center rules about fighting."

"Yeah," Bobbi Joy grumbled. "But they were making fun of me."

"That's not true," Jamie spoke up.

"If you have something you'd like to settle, why don't you do it at the knock hockey table?" Ms. Morgan suggested.

"Yeah," Bobbi Joy said and smiled wickedly.

"Great," Randi said. "Let's go."

We all headed toward the game room where there was bumper pool, ping pong, miniature hockey, and knock hockey.

We played knock hockey on a board designed like a small ice hockey rink. At opposite ends there were goal nets. Each player used a small, wooden hockey stick to hit a rubber puck into the other player's goal.

"Where are you going?" Sylvia Rumsford asked as we walked past.

"Bobbi Joy challenged Randi to a knock hockey game," I said.

"Grudge match!" Sylvia called out.

Billy Parker came running up with Chris Miles. "Who's playing a grudge match?" Billy asked.

"Randi and Bobbi Joy," Sylvia explained.

"Grudge match," Billy called out.

By the time we reached the game room there was a crowd around us.

Bobbi Joy and Randi took their positions at opposite ends of the table. Ms. Morgan picked up the puck as Jamie, I, and the rest of the kids formed a big circle around them.

"You both know the rules," Ms. Morgan said. "So, let's play."

Randi's hands moved like lightning. She whacked the puck and it bounced off the side and right into Bobbi Joy's net.

"One to zero, Randi," Ms. Morgan announced as Bobbi fumed and popped the puck out of her net. "Remember, whoever gets three goals first wins the game."

This time Bobbi Joy was faster. She hit the puck but Randi blocked the shot. Randi fired it back.

"Yeah, Randi!" Chris Miles shouted, but Bobbi Joy blocked the puck. She whacked her stick extra hard, slamming into Randi's hand.

"Ouch!" Randi cried out.

"Oh, so sorry," Bobbi laughed.

Randi didn't answer. Instead, she hit a hard shot and it skidded right into Bobbi Joy's goal.

"Two to zero in favor of Randi," announced Ms. Morgan.

"Good shot, Randi," I said. She grinned back at me.

"Ready? Play!" Ms. Morgan said again. Bobbi Joy took a wild swing at the puck. It zoomed across the table and missed Randi's goal. It hit the back wall and bounced all the way back toward Bobbi Joy's goal and into her net. The game was over!

"Three to zero, Randi wins," Ms. Morgan announced as Bobbi Joy stormed off.

"Thanks, Bobbi," said Randi. "I enjoyed it."

"Good game, Randi," Billy Parker said as the crowd started to break up.

"See you later," Ms. Morgan said. "I've got to check downstairs to make sure the stage is ready for tomorrow."

I gulped, hoping that there was going to be a show.

"What are we going to do now?" Jamie asked us.

"I guess go home," Randi said.

"Now that you had your big entrance in a limo, you want to go home," I teased her.

"Sure," she said, grinning back.

"I'll walk with you," Jamie said.

We walked out of the rec center just as a new song began playing through the intercom system. It was Eric's song, *Hometown Girl.*

During the walk home, Jamie quizzed us about our day with Eric. I was glad when we dropped Jamie off at her house. Randi and I needed answers ourselves—about how to help Eric and Derrick. And we just couldn't talk about their situation in front of Jamie.

"Have you come up with any ideas about how to help Eric?" Randi asked as she opened our front door. I shook my head.

"Hey! What's that?" I asked. Then I realized it was Eric's new song that had been playing at the rec center.

We followed the music into the living room, where Randi and I saw that Eric's tape was playing in Trouble's portable cassette player. The strangest sight, though, was Dad and Trouble dancing around the coffee table. They both looked so funny that we started to giggle.

Teddy held Hoppy in one hand and a little spoon

in the other. Dad held a wooden tablespoon. Both of them were pretending that the spoons were microphones. They were mouthing the words to the song like they were doing the singing.

Dad finally stopped dancing and clicked off the tape player.

"I didn't know you were a singer, Dad," I teased him.

"Teddy and I were having a little fun."

"Yeah. We having fun!" Teddy exclaimed. "Hoppy loves rock-a-roll moosick."

"So, Dad, when are you entering your first lip-synching contest?" Randi asked.

"It's just for fun," he said, looking a little embarrassed.

"That's it!" I practically screamed at her. "That's our answer."

"Lip-synching," Randi repeated. "Yeah, that could be it. Ya-hoo!"

"We good," Teddy said and grinned.

"Yeah, we must be," Dad said. "Or they wouldn't be screaming and jumping up and down."

CHAPTER Ten

"GOME clown girl. She's a gome clown girl,"
Teddy sang as we drove up to the rec center
early the next morning.

"Teddy, please stop singing that," I said.

"And put down that dumb lunch box," Randi
added.

Teddy was holding onto his Super Hog lunch
box like it held the last peanut butter and jelly
sandwich in the world. Super Hog was Teddy's
favorite cartoon character.

"No," said Teddy as he clutched his lunch box
even tighter. Then he started singing again.

"Mom, why did you let Teddy bring that lunch
box? It's so embarrassing," Randi groaned.

109

"If Teddy is going to sit around all day, he'd better have a snack to keep him busy," Mom said.

"He could have used a paper bag," Randi replied.

"Stop picking on Teddy," Dad told Randi. "He packed a snack all by himself."

Randi sighed. "You're right, Dad. Sorry, Trouble. I guess I'm nervous about everything going okay today," she said.

"You'll do fine," I assured her. "We worked out most of the kinks last night."

"Yeah, we did," Randi agreed.

"Is that why you called Mr. Starr last night?" Mom asked.

"Yeah, we had a few problems at rehearsal yesterday," I explained.

"What kind of problems?" Dad asked.

"Uh, technical stuff," Randi answered quickly. "It's difficult to explain."

"Here we are," Dad said as we pulled into the parking lot. He pulled up behind the video trucks. Beside them were two vans and the big R.V. where we'd met Derrick. A few men were pulling cables from the trucks into the rec center's basement.

"Mr. Starr is waiting for us," I said as I opened the back door and jumped out. "We'll see you inside."

"See you," said Teddy.

"Check in with us before the concert," Dad said.

"Okay," Randi agreed as we headed toward the R.V.

James was standing guard.

"Good morning, James," Randi greeted.

"Morning, girls," James answered. "Go on inside. Everyone is waiting for you."

"Thanks," I said.

Mr. Starr, Ms. Brown, Marty, Eric, and Derrick were all there.

"Good morning," I said, trying to sound cheerful.

"Morning," Eric replied glumly. "I was hoping that I wouldn't be as scared today, but I am."

"Randi, last night on the phone you said you had an idea that involved lip-synching," Mr. Starr said. "Tell us what you had in mind."

"Okay," Randi said as she sat down. "Sandi

and I don't know exactly how to do this, but Eric could do the singing and Derrick could do the performing."

"What?" Eric asked, looking at us as if we were crazy.

I explained about how Dad and Teddy used spoons as microphones and danced around the living room pretending to be rock stars.

"Eric can sing, but he doesn't want to be on stage," I said. "And Derrick likes to be on stage but he doesn't sing as well as Eric does. So if Eric could somehow sing behind the stage or somewhere, he wouldn't have to be in front of the crowd."

A big smile spread across Mr. Starr's face. "Hey, Marty, I bet we could rig up a sound and monitor system in here."

"Yeah, it'd be easy," Marty told him. "Eric could watch the monitor in here and see what Derrick was doing on stage. He could make sure he sings at the right pace."

"What about the microphones?" Ms. Brown asked.

"Derrick's microphone would be working only when he talks to the crowd between songs," Marty explained. "I'll be sure it's off whenever Eric is singing. And the whole thing can be coordinated from out here in the truck."

Mr. Starr looked at the St. John twins.

"What do you two think about the idea?" he asked.

Derrick grinned. "I think it's a great idea," he said. "I know the words to Eric's songs. So that's no problem."

Eric shrugged his shoulders. "Yeah, I'm sure we could do it," he agreed. "But do you think the kids will really be fooled?"

Mr. Starr thought about it for a second. "Yeah, I'm sure no one will be able to tell," he said. "The band will be playing live and the kids will be screaming and cheering. I think we're pretty safe with this."

"Thanks to Sandi and Randi," Ms. Brown said.

"Uh, there is still one more problem," Randi spoke up.

"What?" Mr. Starr asked.

"Sandi won't go on stage for me," she said.

"Why not?" Eric asked.

"Because Randi won the dream date contest, not me," I told him. "It wouldn't be fair if I was in the video and she wasn't. And besides that, my parents can tell us apart and they'll be in the audience. I don't want to get into big trouble again."

"So why don't you and Randi do the same thing?" Derrick suggested. "Randi can go on stage and you can sing here in the R.V. with Eric."

"Do you think you can lip-synch the song, Randi?" Mr. Starr asked.

Randi beamed. "Sure I can," she said eagerly.

"How about it, Sandi?" Mr. Starr asked me.

"Let's do it," I agreed.

"Then we'll need to pick another person to dance in the video onstage," Ms. Brown said.

"Every kid out there wants to be in the video," Mr. Starr said. "Finding someone shouldn't be too hard."

"Let Randi pick someone," Eric suggested.

"Okay," Ms. Brown agreed.

"Let's get to work," Marty said. "I need to set up the microphones and video stuff in here."

"Derrick, you and Randi report to the makeup person in twenty minutes," Mr. Starr said. "Sandi, you'd better go tell your parents where you'll be. And Eric, you stay here and relax. The problems are solved."

Eric smiled.

"Okay, everyone," Mr. Starr said. "Let's get busy and make *Hometown Girl* into the most exciting music video ever!"

"Yeah!" we all cheered as we headed outside and into the rec center. This sure was going to be a crazy day—and one that we'd probably remember for a long, long time.

CHAPTER Eleven

RANDI and I weaved our way around the busy workers and onto the stage. We quickly spotted Mom and Dad talking to Ms. Morgan. Teddy was sitting on the floor clutching his Super Hog lunch box.

I looked around the room. There was activity everywhere. Technicians were setting up cameras and lights. The guys in Eric's band were making some kind of adjustments to their musical equipment. And in the far corner, Ms. Brown was talking to Jamie and the other dancers for the video.

"Don't forget," I told Randi. "You have to pick someone to take my place on stage."

"That won't be hard," Randi said. "Most of the

kids in town are dying to be in it."

I nodded. "We'd better go over and tell Mom and Dad what's going on," I suggested. "We have lots to do."

"Okay," Randi agreed.

"Well, here come the local stars now," said Ms. Morgan when she saw us walking over.

Randi smiled.

"Is everything solved now?" Dad asked us.

"Yep," Randi said.

"We've got the best seats in the house," Mom said, pointing to the front row. "We'll be able to see everything from there."

Suddenly, Teddy cried out. "Every rock-a-roll fan be here," he said.

"Well, almost every fan will be here," I said. "I'll be outside working in the van."

"Why?" Dad asked.

"Mr. Starr asked if I could help him do some behind-the-scenes stuff," I explained.

"But Sandi," said Mom, "then you won't be in the video."

"I don't mind, Mom," I assured her. "I'll be in it in a different way."

"You really don't mind?" Dad asked.

I shook my head.

"Well, okay," he said.

"Is there anything else we should know?" Mom asked, giving us a funny look. Sometimes I thought she could read our minds.

"Uh, I get to wear makeup!" Randi announced quickly, changing the subject.

Dad folded his arms and stared at Randi. Then he smiled.

"Wearing makeup twice in one week," he said. "I guess my girls are growing up. But don't get used to it. The rules still stand."

Randi nodded as Ms. Brown joined our group.

"Randi, it's almost time for you to get ready," she said. "Before you go to makeup though, who have you picked to take Sandi's place on stage?"

"I don't know," Randi said and shrugged. I saw her look down at Teddy. "How about Trouble?"

"No," Dad said, shaking his head. "It's really

119

sweet of you to want your brother in your video, but he's too young."

"Okay," Randi agreed, turning to Ms. Brown. "Could I have a minute to think?"

"Sure," she said.

Randi and I walked over to where Jamie and the other dancers were standing.

"Isn't this just too exciting?" Jamie asked. "Sylvia and I get to dance right beside Eric. I'm glad everything is working out. Everything is okay, isn't it?"

"Yeah," I assured her.

"Relax," Randi said. "Sandi is going to sing off stage. I'll be on stage lip-synching the words."

"Now all I have to do is pick someone to take Sandi's place on stage," said Randi.

"Take your pick," Jamie said, looking around at the zillion kids who were streaming through the rec center doors.

There was cute Cara Smith. Randi shook her head. She didn't like her because she acted stuck up.

"How about Todd?" I whispered.

"Are you kidding?" asked Randi. "He'd probably do something disgusting while Eric was singing and ruin the whole video."

"Then who do you want to be in it?" I asked.

"Bobbi Joy," Randi announced.

"No way!" sputtered Jamie.

"Are you crazy?" I asked. "Why?"

"Because Bobbi Joy wanted to be in the video so badly," Randi explained. "Besides, it'd be fun to shock her. It'll drive her crazy that I'm being so nice to her."

"I guess so," I said, still unconvinced.

"Why would you do something nice for someone who's so mean to you?" Jamie asked.

"Maybe no one has ever done anything nice for Bobbi Joy," Randi said.

I smiled at my sister. "Okay, let's go over and tell her," I said.

"Hi, Bobbi Joy," Randi called to her.

"What do you want?" Bobbi Joy barked at us.

"We want to ask you something," I said.

"What?" she snapped back.

"Would you want to be a dancer in the video?" Randi asked her.

"R-really?" Bobbi Joy sputtered.

"Yes, really," Randi said.

"This isn't a joke or a trick, is it?" Bobbi Joy asked.

"No," Randi said.

"Oh, yes," Bobbi Joy replied. "Thanks."

"Then you'd better go over to Ms. Brown over there," I said. "She'll tell you what you have to do."

"Thanks," Bobbi repeated as she hurried toward Ms. Brown.

Randi and I shook hands and winked at each other.

"You'd better get to makeup," I said.

"And you'd better get out to the truck," Randi said.

"Good luck, sis," I said, giving her a quick hug.

"Thanks, Sandi," Randi said, hugging me back. "Now let's make rock music history."

CHAPTER Twelve

"GREAT, you're here," Marty said as I burst through the door and took my seat in the R.V.

"I'm ready," I said.

"Okay, let me explain things," Marty said to Eric and me, pointing to the monitors. "By watching these screens, you'll be able to see what's happening on stage and behind the stage where Ms. Brown will be. Through these headsets, you'll hear me giving you directions from the truck next door. And you'll also be able to hear the music."

Eric and I nodded.

"Go ahead and try on your headsets," Marty said. "See how they feel."

I picked up my headset and tried it on.

"How do they feel?" Mr. Starr asked.

"Fine," I said.

"Great," said Eric. "It's just like recording in the studio."

"That's the idea," Mr.Starr said and smiled at us. We both took off the headsets.

"Well, it looks like we're almost ready to start," Marty said. "We both better head over to the control truck now and get ourselves set up. We'll talk to you from there and tell you when to begin singing."

He smiled and gave us a thumbs-up sign, then headed out the door.

"Good luck," said Mr. Starr.

"Thanks," Eric and I said together.

As soon as we were alone, we put on our headsets and stared at the monitors. I could see the stage clearly on monitor number one. Derrick was standing in front of the band in a huge spotlight. Randi was standing behind Derrick and off to one side. Jamie, Sylvia, Chris, Billy, and Bobbi Joy were all standing in dimmer spotlights. On another monitor, I could see Ms. Brown and Ms. Morgan. Ms.

Brown was wearing a headset just like the ones we were wearing.

The last two screens showed the stage area and the audience. On one I saw Mom, Dad, and Teddy sitting in the front row. On the other I could see Cara Smith, Todd Jackson, and a bunch of other kids we knew.

I heard a crackle and my headset came to life.

"Eric, can you and Sandi hear me?" Marty asked us from the control truck.

"Loud and clear," Eric replied into his microphone.

"Yeah, fine," I answered.

"Good," said Marty. "Then we won't bother with a formal sound check. I can hear you both well, too. Remember, I'll cue you before it's time to sing. Now I have to talk to Judy and the crew inside the center. You two don't have to worry about any of the stuff we talk about."

I looked at Eric and smiled. He smiled back. Marty told Ms. Brown that he wanted to finish the video as quickly as possible.

"Unless I yell cut," he said, "don't stop the action on stage."

"Okay. You're the director," Ms. Brown answered.

"Go ahead and tell the audience what to do. Then we're ready to roll," Marty said.

Eric and I listened as Ms. Brown told everyone in the audience to act really excited. It seemed pretty stupid to tell them that when I knew they'd all be screaming as soon as the band started to play *Hometown Girl.*

"We're ready," Marty cued us a few minutes later. "*Hometown Girl* video. Take one. Tape rolling. Ten seconds."

The recreation center lights dimmed. "Start the smoke machines." Colored smoke began to drift across the stage. "Now add the lights," Marty said. Multicolored lights suddenly lit up the stage. "Okay, now. Three, two, one, and music."

We watched as Ms. Brown pointed to the band to begin. As soon as they played the first note, the crowd started to scream and dance. It was really exciting to watch. I was thrilled to be a part of it—

even if nobody knew what kind of part I had.

"Cue the dancers," Marty called.

Ms. Brown pointed to Jamie, Sylvia, and the others. They started to dance. I quickly checked the other screens. I saw Mom, Dad, and Teddy in their seats. They were swaying to the beat.

And then I noticed that Teddy was opening his lunch box. Even though he was just a little kid, it seemed like a strange time to eat a snack.

"Turn on the stage spotlights," Marty said. "Get ready to sing in the R.V., Eric. Kill the stage microphone. Okay, now, ready and sing."

"Hometown Girl," Eric sang loudly and perfectly on key. "You're my hometown pearl. There's no other in the world like my hometown girl."

While Eric sang, I watched the monitor. Derrick was doing a super job of lip-synching the words. It was almost impossible to tell that he wasn't singing. He was looking at Randi and pretending to sing his heart out.

Suddenly, Marty spoke to me. "Your part is coming up Sandi," he said. "Get ready. On the beat. Now do it."

I took a deep breath and belted out my part. "You're my hometown boy," I sang. "You are my pride and joy."

As I finished my part, Eric sang again. I looked at the monitor. I saw Mom and Dad giving each other weird looks. That meant they knew that I was singing for Randi. We'd have some explaining to do later.

Then I noticed that Teddy was jumping out of his seat. His lunch box was open wide and he was holding on to Hoppy. I gulped. Teddy had sneaked Hoppy into the concert in his lunch box! I crossed my fingers, hoping that Trouble and Hoppy wouldn't ruin the video.

Just then, the band began playing louder than ever. For a minute I lost sight of Teddy. The crowd was really going wild. I searched the screens—and finally I spotted him. He was running up the steps and onto the stage.

Teddy held on to Hoppy and started doing his crazy dance that he liked to do around the coffee table at home.

Eric looked at me. I shrugged my shoulders. There was nothing I could do.

"Do you want to cut it so I can get the kid and his frog off the stage?" I heard Ms. Brown ask Marty.

"No, keep going," Marty said. "The crowd is getting into it and we don't want to calm everybody down and start all over again. We'll edit out the kid later." Marty paused. "Get ready for the second verse, Eric. Three, two, one. Now hit it!"

I couldn't take my eyes off Teddy while Eric sang. Teddy was parading around the stage like a pint-sized dancer. Why did Teddy always ruin things for Randi and me?

As Eric sang the last word and the band stopped, Marty yelled to stop the tape.

"Cut!" Ms. Brown repeated. The lights went on and the audience relaxed. Some kids started talking and giggling, while others sat down. Everyone on stage had stopped dancing except Teddy.

"Theodore Michael Daniels!" Randi roared as she raced toward him. I could hear her through

Ms. Brown's headset.

"This time you've gone too far!" Mom said, as she and Dad raced up on stage.

"It's okay," Ms. Brown said. "Mr. Starr kind of liked it. He said it gave the video a real hometown feel."

I took off my headset and looked at Eric.

"Did I hear right?" I asked. "Did Ms. Brown say Mr. Starr liked everything . . . including Teddy and his stupid frog?"

"Yeah, that's what he said," Eric said and grinned.

"Let's try another take," Marty said. "But this time let's keep the boy off stage. Okay?"

"Right, Marty," Ms. Brown agreed.

"Don't worry," I heard Dad say. "This time Teddy and Hoppy will be sitting on my lap."

"Dat no fun," Teddy groaned loudly. "Hoppy love rock-a-roll moosic. He gome clown girl."

Eric laughed.

"Everyone, please get back in your places," Ms. Brown called to the audience. "Let's do it one more time, okay? Ready? Three, two, one . . ."

CHAPTER Thirteen

W E did the whole video three more times. I was tired and I hadn't even done any of the dancing.

"That's a wrap," Marty said at last, meaning that everyone was done.

"Phew! That was hard work," I said to Eric as I took off my headset. Eric nodded and took off his headset.

"Thanks, Sandi. Derrick and I appreciate all your help. You saved the video," Eric said.

Eric really was sweet. I liked him a lot.

"You're going to be a big star," I told him. "And pretty soon you'll get over being nervous in front of crowds."

133

"But until I do, you and Randi will keep our secret, won't you?" Eric asked with a wink.

"It's a promise," I said, "from one twin to another." I reached out and shook Eric's hand. "Now I'd better go and explain to my folks about this singing thing."

"Just one more thing," Eric said, looking deep into my eyes. He leaned over and kissed me on the cheek. It was the first time a boy had ever kissed me. I knew it was just a thank-you kiss, but I was thrilled. A big star had kissed me! I could feel my cheeks turning bright red.

"Bye, Eric," I said as I covered my cheek with my hand and jumped up. I opened the door and hopped out.

"Bye, Sandi," he said. "I'll write to you."

"That would be great," I said.

Inside the rec center I saw that Derrick was signing autographs for a group of fans. He waved as I walked by. I noticed that Bobbi Joy held out her arm for Derrick to sign it.

"Oh, I'll never wash my arm again," Bobbi

Joy told him.

I looked around the room and spotted Mom, Dad, and Teddy. They were standing on the other side of the stage with Randi and Jamie.

"Hi, everyone," I greeted as I walked up to the group.

"You were great, Sandi," Randi said as she and Jamie hugged me.

"You guys were great, too," I said.

"I great," Teddy said. "Hoppy, too." Trouble proudly held up his frog.

"It's time for Hoppy to go back in the lunch box," said Dad. He opened Teddy's Super Hog lunch box and placed Hoppy inside. "And it's also time to hear about this singing switcheroo."

"Don't be angry, Mr. Daniels," Mr. Starr said as he walked up to us. "If Randi and Sandi hadn't jumped in to help us, there wouldn't have been a video today."

Mr. Starr told Dad about Melanie and her illness. By the time he'd finished the story, Dad was smiling.

"And, Dad, we really didn't pull a switcheroo," I spoke up. "I just sang for Randi. We didn't switch places."

"Yeah, Dad," Randi said.

"Well, I'm proud that you girls offered to help," Mom said.

Dad nodded. "I'm proud of you, too. But how would you all feel if you had twins who switched places all the time?"

Mr. Starr coughed. I looked at Randi and we burst out in giggles.

"What's so funny?" Jamie asked.

"Oh, nothing," Randi said quickly.

"You two sure are acting weird," Jamie said.

"We're allowed to act weird," I said. "We were just on a dream date with Eric St. John."

"Dweeb date! Dweeb date!" yelled Teddy as he jumped up and down.

Derrick finished signing autographs and joined us.

"I'll miss Trouble," he said, grinning. "What a great little brother!"

Randi and I groaned together.

◆ ◆ ◆ ◆ ◆

For the next week, all everyone at school talked about was Eric St. John and his video. They were dying for the video to air on TV so they could catch glimpses of themselves.

Randi was treated like a queen for about three days. Then, suddenly, she wasn't a celebrity anymore. Bobbi Joy was mean to us again and Todd the Cod stopped offering to carry Randi's books to class.

Eric's *Hometown Girl* zoomed up the music charts and soon was one of the most popular records on the radio. Then, one morning, about two weeks after Eric and Derrick left, Mr. Starr called Mom and Dad. He said the video would be shown on TV that night.

It was hard to pay attention during school. Kids and teachers were excited about the video. Even Bobbi Joy was pretty nice to us. Finally, the last bell of the day rang and everybody cheered.

To celebrate, Dad brought home hamburgers, fries, and milkshakes for supper. We all gathered around the TV to eat and watch the *Hometown Girl* video.

"Thanks for inviting me over," Jamie said as she took a slurp of her milkshake.

"I can't wait to see the video," Mom said. "It'll be a riot to see if Sandi's singing goes with Randi's mouth."

"I a star," Teddy exclaimed as he jumped up onto Mom's lap.

"Teddy, you might not be in the video," I warned.

"I da star," Teddy insisted.

"Maybe Trouble will see himself in the audience," Randi said.

"Yeah, maybe," I agreed.

Just then, the phone rang.

"I get it," yelled Teddy as he bounded off Mom's lap. "I get da phone!" He zoomed by and almost stepped in my food.

"Sanee! Ranee! Da phone!" Trouble called to

me a minute later.

"Tell whoever it is that we'll call back," Randi said.

"No, don't," I called. "I'll get it."

I raced toward Teddy and grabbed the phone.

"Hello," I said. "This is Sandi."

"Hi, Sandi!" a familiar voice said. "Remember me?"

"I can't believe it! Hi, Eric!" I said. "It's great to hear from you. Randi and I wrote you a letter. Did you get it?"

"Yep," Eric said. "Derrick says hi to you both. And he especially wanted to thank Randi for her hot tips on playing the old switcheroo trick on people."

I laughed. "If Derrick uses Randi's tips, he'll probably get into big trouble. We always do."

"I just called to tell you to watch tonight's video. It turned out great! Ken and Marty are really happy about it," Eric said. "The ending is really wild. I think your family will enjoy it."

"We're all sitting around waiting for it to start," I said.

"It should be on in a minute or so. I'd better go. Please keep in touch, Sandi," Eric said and hung up.

"Hurry up, Sandi," Randi called. "It's coming on."

I put down the phone and raced back to my seat. I got there just as the video began.

"Look, there I am!" cried Jamie excitedly. "And there's Sylvia, Chris, Billy, and Bobbi Joy."

"Eric sounds great," Dad said as he tapped his toe in time to the music.

"And there I am in the audience," said Mom.

"Look at Todd the Cod," Randi said, pointing at the screen.

"There you are, Randi," Dad said as the camera moved in for a closeup of her.

"Do I look okay?" she asked nervously.

"You look beautiful," Dad said. "And Sandi sounds great. It's amazing how well you two pulled that off."

"Who was on the phone?" Mom asked.

"It was Eric St. John," I said. "He said that Marty and Mr. Starr were really happy with the way the video turned out. And he said something about the ending being great."

"Where's Hoppy?" Teddy asked impatiently.

"It's not over yet," I said, crossing my fingers and hoping my brother was in an audience shot somewhere.

At the end of the video we saw Eric's surprise. It was Teddy—and Hoppy. They both were dancing across the stage. They hadn't cut that scene after all.

"I da star," Teddy said proudly, touching the TV screen. "I da star of gome clown girl."

"You sure are," Dad chuckled.

"And you're my dream date," I said as I hugged my little brother.

"No, he's my dream date," said Randi as she hugged Teddy, too.

"I notta dweeb date," protested Teddy. "Eric da dweeb date."

Teddy jumped up and began wiggling his way across the living room. We all broke up into giggles.

About the Author

MICHAEL J. PELLOWSKI was born January 24, 1949, in New Brunswick, New Jersey. He is a graduate of Rutgers, the State University of New Jersey, and has a degree in education. Before turning to writing, Michael was a professional football player and then a high school teacher.

Michael has written more than 125 books for children. When he's not writing books, Michael enjoys fishing with his family, as well as jogging and exercising.